2222222222222

3333333333333

44444444444444

2222222222222222

3333333333333

444444444444444

WHAT COMES IN

2's, 3's, & 4's?

By Suzanne Aker

Illustrated by Bernie Karlin

Simon and Schuster Books for Young Readers   Published by Simon & Schuster Inc.   New York

Simon & Schuster
Books for Young Readers

Simon & Schuster Building
Rockefeller Center
1230 Avenue of the Americas
New York, New York 10020

SIMON & SCHUSTER BOOKS FOR YOUNG READERS
is a trademark of Simon & Schuster.

Designed by Bernie Karlin
Manufactured in the United States of America
10 9 8 7 6 5 4 3 2
(pbk)   10 9 8 7 6 5 4 3 2

Library of Congress Cataloging-in-Publication Data

Aker, Suzanne.

What comes in 2's, 3's and 4's?

Summary: Introduces the numbers two, three,
and four, by enumerating the ways in which they occur
in everyday life, from your two eyes and two arms
to the four seasons of the year.

1. Counting—Juvenile literature.   [1. Number concept.
2. Counting.]   I. Karlin, Bernie, ill.
II. Title.   III. Title: What comes in twos, threes, and fours?
QA113.A52   1990   [E]   89-35482
ISBN: 0-671-67173-1   ISBN: 0-671-79247-4 (pbk)

WHAT COMES IN
2's, 3's, & 4's?

To my three grandsons,
Aaron, Anthony,
and Trent — S.A.

To my wife, Mati — B.K.

WHAT COMES IN 2's?

Just look at you!
You have
2 eyes,
2 ears,
2 arms,
2 hands,
2 legs,
and
2 feet.

And when you look in the mirror, there are **2** of you.

There are **2** handles on the sink –
one hot and one cold.

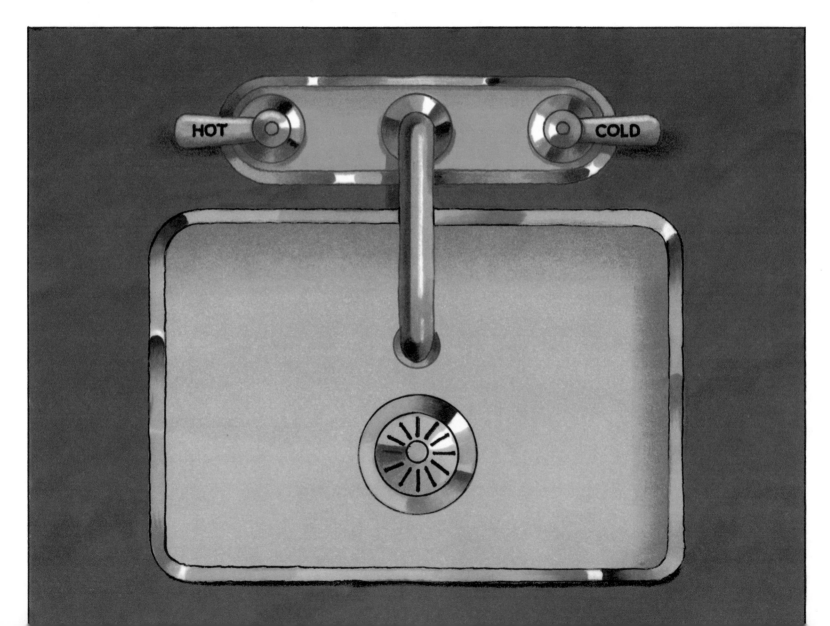

There are **2** pieces of bread
on the sandwich.

There are **2** ways to go on a seesaw – up…

and down.

Birds
have
2 wings.

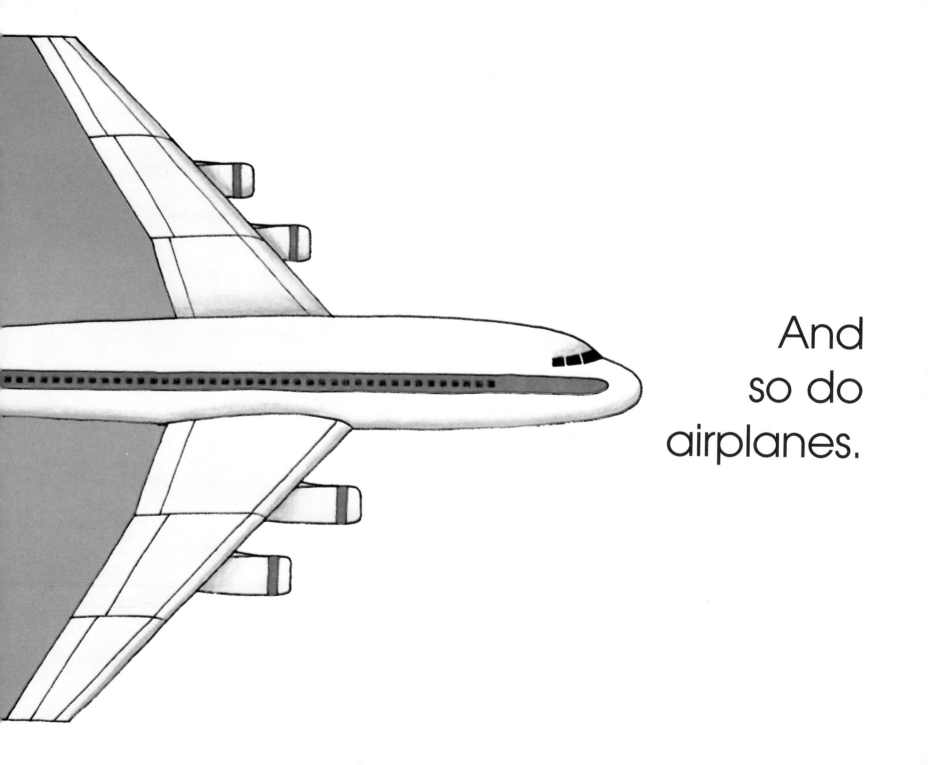

And
so do
airplanes.

There are **2** pillows on the bed.

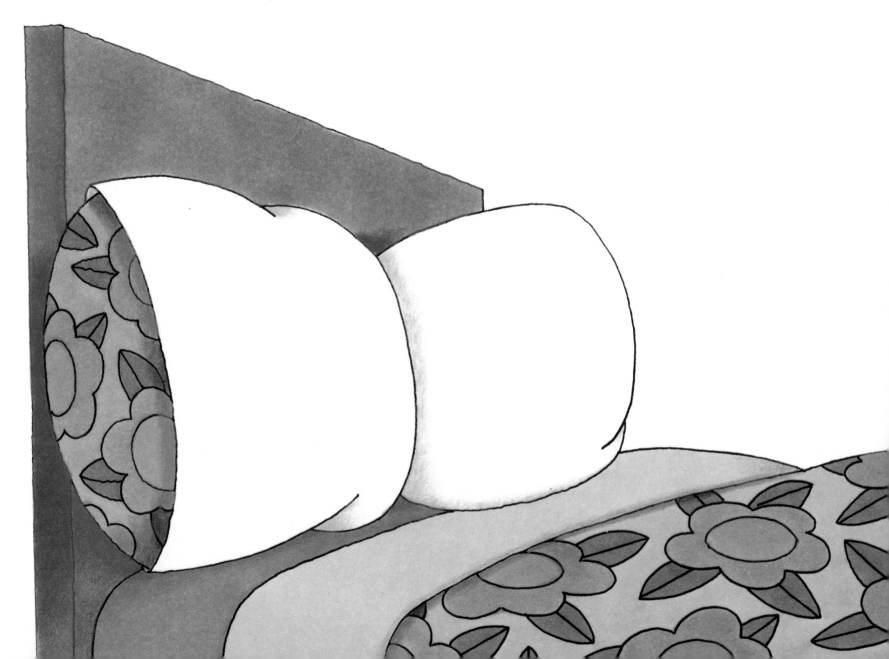

And **2** teddy bears waiting for you to say good night.

WHAT COMES IN 3's?

Traffic signals have **3** lights – red for stop,

yellow for slow,

and green for go.

There are **3** wheels on a tricycle.

We have **3** meals each day –

breakfast,	lunch,	and dinner.

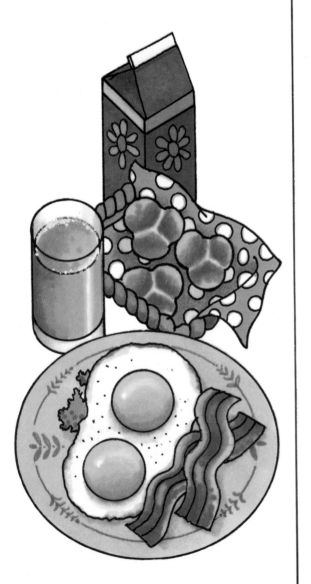 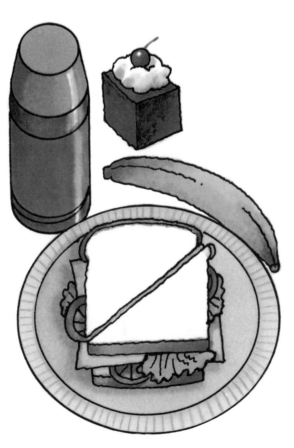 

Here are **3** things that help us to eat –
a knife, a fork, and a spoon.

Most things come in **3** sizes –
small,   medium,   and large.

There are **3** colors you can mix to make other colors – red, yellow, and blue.

These are **3** important shapes –
a circle,   a square,

and a triangle.

There are **3** sides to a slice of pizza.

And **3** leaves on poison ivy —
watch out!

WHAT COMES IN 4's?

There are **4** wheels on mommy's car.

And **4** wheels on my wagon.

The chair has **4** legs and so does the table

So does the cat

and so does the dog.

There are
4 panes of glass
in the window.

And **4** places to cook on the stove.

There are **4** seasons in the year – spring,

summer, fall, winter

And there are
4 corners on this book.

Can you count them?

2222222222222
3333333333333
444444444444

222222222222222
333333333333
44444444444444